D0858272

FIC	Willis, Connie, auth
WIL	
	Take a look at the f
	ive and ten.

LEXINGTON COUNTY PUBLIC LIBRARY
Cayce-West Columbia Branch Library
1500 Augusta Road
West Columbia, SC 29169

Connie Willis

Connie Willis

THIS SPECIAL SIGNED EDITION is limited to 1500 numbered copies.

This is copy 1332

Take a Look at the
at the
Five and Ten

Take a Look at the Five and Ten

CONNIE WILLIS

SUBTERRANEAN PRESS 2020

Take a Look at the Five and Ten
Copyright © 2020 by Connie Willis.
All rights reserved.

Dust jacket and interior illustrations
Copyright © 2020 by Jon Foster.
All rights reserved.

Interior design Copyright © 2020
by Desert Isle Design, LLC. All rights reserved.

First Edition

ISBN
978-1-64524-019-8

Subterranean Press
PO Box 190106
Burton, MI 48519

subterraneanpress.com

Manufactured in the United States of America

"Repeat the sounding joy!"
"Joy to the World"

EVERYBODY HAS A TRAUMATIC Christmas memory, and mine was always Christmas dinner, partly because in my family (a term used *very* loosely), it's actually a series of dinners— Thanksgiving dinner, Christmas dinner, and a New Year's Eve buffet, and if my one-time stepfather Dave had his way, we'd also have St. Lucia's Day and Boxing Day and Twelfth Night dinners, and who knows what else.

He's very big on family gatherings, even though he's been married at least half a dozen times and has terrible taste in women (including where my mother was concerned), which means he thinks of me as his daughter, even though he was only married to her for about fifteen minutes back when I was eight and is always really nice to me, even to the extent of helping me with college, so it's hard for me to say no to coming.

I'm not the only sort-of-relative he invites. There's also Aunt Mildred, actually a great-aunt of Dave's second wife, and Grandma Elving, the grandmother of his fourth. Got all that straight?

Also at the dinner are Dave's current wife Jillian (another bad marital choice), her stuck-up daughter Sloane, Sloane's boyfriend of the moment, who is always blond and tall and going to law school or med school, and Jillian's equally stuck-up friends, who Jillian introduces Aunt Mildred, Grandma Elving, and me to by saying, "Dave is so kind. He wants to make sure everyone has someplace to go for the holidays!" as if we were people he'd picked up on the sidewalk outside a homeless shelter or something.

Add to that the fact that Jillian refuses to have roast turkey and pumpkin pie like normal people and insists on serving poached sturgeon and Senegalese locus-pods, that Aunt Mildred complains about everything from the table settings to my failure to bring a date, and that Grandma

Elving insists on telling the same interminable story of how she worked at Woolworth's in downtown Denver one Christmas, and you can see why I start dreading Thanksgiving dinner some time in July.

This year was no exception. Jillian met me at the door with a look that said clearly, "Why didn't you use the servant's entrance?" and the news that I needed to go pick up Grandma Elving. "Dave's on a conference call, and he doesn't think she should be driving."

"Couldn't I go get her instead?" Sloane's boyfriend said to me. He was named Lassiter this year and was even taller and blonder than usual.

"Oh, no, Lassiter, I couldn't let you do that," Jillian said. "You're a guest. Ori can go." She turned to me. "And on the way, pick up ice and some turmeric."

"And don't drive Grandma Elving anywhere near downtown on the way back," Sloane said. "I don't want her telling that stupid Woolworth's story again."

"Woolworth's?" Lassiter asked.

"It was a dime store," I explained, "a kind of variety store, like—"

"The Dollar Store," Sloane said, putting her hand possessively on Lassiter's arm. "She worked there one Christmas back in the fifties when she was 'a girl,' and we have to listen to her go on about it every single year."

"Really?" he said. "That's interesting."

"No, it's not," Sloane said. "It's boring beyond belief, so, Ori, whatever you do, don't mention Christmas shopping or snow."

"Or Bing Crosby," Jillian put in.

"Oh, God, yes, especially don't mention Bing Crosby. Or lunch counters or nativity scenes." She turned to Lassiter. "And if she starts in, don't encourage her. She can go on for hours. Just ignore her. Or change the subject." She turned back to me. "Do not say *anything* to her on the way here that'll set her off."

That was easier said than done. Almost anything, from buses to the weather, reminded her of it. Even the traffic lights. "Look at them, turning from red to green," she said after I'd picked her up from her retirement community apartment. "They look so festive, almost like Christmas decorations themselves. I remember that Christmas I worked at Woolworth's getting off work and seeing them, blinking red and green on Sixteenth Street."

"Jillian asked me to pick up a few things on our way back," I said, pulling into Safeway. "Is there anything you want?"

"No," she said. "I don't suppose they'd have hot roasted nuts? They sold hot salted peanuts and cashews at Woolworth's from this little red-and-white striped cart. It had a yellow heat lamp in it to keep the nuts warm, and little paper bags to scoop them into."

"I'll see. Will you be warm enough sitting here?" I asked, looking at her doubtfully. She was bundled up in a black cloth coat and a gray scarf and gloves, but she was awfully thin and frail-looking, and my car heater doesn't work all that well.

"Oh, I'll be fine," she said. "This is much warmer than that bus I used to take that Christmas I worked at Woolworth's. It was so cold the windows used to frost over and—"

I fled into the store, grabbed the ice and the turmeric and hurried back out, hoping she'd forgotten about the roasted nuts.

She had. She was looking at the Santa Claus collecting money for charity outside Safeway's main door. "That Christmas I worked at Woolworth's there was a Santa right outside the front door. He had a cotton-wool beard and a chimney you put the money in. It was made out of—"

"Aunt Mildred's going to be at dinner," I said, trying to change the topic. "And Sloane and her new boyfriend Lassiter and Stan and Louise Devers—"

"Is he cute?" Grandma Elving asked. "Or whatever it is you girls call it nowadays?"

"Stan Devers?" He was at least fifty and completely bald.

"No, Sloane's boyfriend," she said. "Is he cute? And more importantly, is he nice?"

"Yes," I said, even though I was basing that solely on his having offered to pick up Grandma Elving and the fact that he'd spoken to me at all. None of Sloane's boyfriends had ever so much as asked me if I wanted some more salad, though last year it had been distressed kale with anchovies, so that was no loss.

"Lassiter," she repeated thoughtfully. "There was a boy named Lamar who worked in the music department at Woolworth's that Christmas. They sold record players and 45s and guitar picks," and she was off again.

Dinner was just as bad. Mrs. Devers said, "What a lovely table, Jillian!" and Grandma Elving piped up, "Your tablecloth looks just like the ones we used to sell at Woolworth's. They were white with poinsettias embroidered on them, and they came in a set with eight napkins for $2.99."

Jillian, who'd never paid $2.99 for anything in her life, looked offended, and Sloane leaned across the table to whisper to me, "I thought I told you not to let her get started on Woolworth's, Ori."

"In my day," Aunt Mildred said, glaring at me, "we were taught it was rude to carry on private conversations at the table," and launched into a diatribe on the current decline in table manners and in civility in general.

When she paused to take a breath, Jillian said, "So, Lassiter, Sloane tells me you're in medical school."

"Yes, at C.U.," he said.

"Ori goes to C.U., too," Dave said.

"You do?" Lassiter said. "What are you majoring in?"

"Lassiter's going to be a neuroscientist," Sloane interrupted. "He's working with Dr. Riordan on a *major* project. Tell them about it, Lassiter. It involves memory, doesn't it?"

"Memory's such a strange thing," Grandma Elving said musingly. "I can remember that Christmas I worked at Woolworth's like it was yesterday."

Uh-oh, there she goes again, I thought, and started to say, "This venison carpaccio is delicious, Jillian," (a lie) but Sloane had beaten me to the punch.

"Lassiter works all the time," she said. "I practically had to tie him down and threaten him with violence to get him to take two weeks off and go skiing with me in Vail. We're going up tomorrow."

"You young people, always running around," Aunt Mildred said disapprovingly. "In *my* day young people stayed put."

"*I* didn't," Grandma Elving said. "That Christmas at Woolworth's I worked in a different department almost every day—Leather Goods, the cosmetic counter, the music department selling 45s, Perry Como and Rosemary Clooney and Bing Crosby. Woolworth's piped in music, too. I can remember them playing 'Silver Bells' and 'It's Beginning to Look a Lot Like Christmas' and—"

"Ori, have you found a job yet?" Sloane cut in, trying to head Grandma Elving off (and remind everybody that I, unlike her, had to work during Christmas break).

"No, not yet. I have an interview tomorrow with—"

"Young people today don't even know what work is," Aunt Mildred interrupted. "In *my* day—"

"What else do you remember about that Christmas besides the music, Mrs. Elving?" Lassiter interrupted. "As you came into the store?" and Sloane looked like she wanted to throttle him.

He *won't be at Christmas dinner*, I thought.

"Do you remember what it smelled like when you walked into the store?" he prompted.

"Oh, my, yes," Grandma Elving said. "Roasted nuts and fudge and popcorn. And pine from the Christmas tree by the door."

"Lassiter—" Sloane said warningly, but he was oblivious.

"What else do you remember?" he asked.

"The store had silver garlands wrapped around the pillars and red-and-green bells, you know, the kind made of pleated paper that fold out, and—"

"Is everyone ready for dessert?" Jillian asked brightly. "It's lychees flambé."

Grandma Elving didn't hear her. "The store windows had artificial snow around the edges and Christmas lights strung across the top, and they were always steamed up."

Lassiter didn't hear Jillian either, even when she told me to go tell the maid to bring dessert in. "You said you could hear Christmas music playing," he persisted. "Can you remember hearing other sounds?"

"Oh, my yes, the shoppers talking and the cash registers ringing up sales and Santa Claus ringing his bell across the street...oh, and the traffic. They had cars on Sixteenth Avenue then, and—"

It took the arrival of flaming pyres of lychees and Aunt Mildred's subsequent remarks on fire danger to bring them to a stop.

"What were you thinking?" Sloane whispered to Lassiter as the after-dinner coffee (balsamic espresso) was being poured. "I told you, she can go on for hours."

"Really?" he said, looking thoughtfully over at Grandma Elving, and I was afraid he was going to go over and ask her what else she remembered, but he didn't, and we got to spend the rest of the evening discussing the comparative merits of Aspen, Vail, and Snowmass for skiing and how people nowadays didn't know how to make a decent cup of coffee and why didn't I have a job yet—or a boyfriend.

"Can't you find one for her, Sloane?" Mrs. Devers asked. "You know *lots* of young men. There must be one who—"

She didn't finish the sentence, but it was clear what she'd intended to say: "One who's not too picky, who wouldn't mind going out with an unemployed shirt-tail relative who can't get a boyfriend of her own."

An absolutely delightful beginning to the Christmas season. I could hardly wait for Christmas.

I used taking the coffee cups to the kitchen as a way to go get my things from the guest bedroom, so I could sneak out and at least not get stuck taking Grandma Elving home, which would be a perfect ending to a perfect night, but as I was putting on my boots, Lassiter came in. "Can I talk to you for a minute?" he asked, pulling the door shut behind him.

"Umm, sure," I said, astonished that one of Sloane's boyfriends had actually registered the fact I existed, let alone wanted to talk to me, and a little flustered. He was so, in Grandma Elving's word, cute.

"Good. It's about your grandmother."

Oh, well, I knew it was too good to be true. "She's not actually my grandmother," I said, yanking on the other boot. "She's my stepfather's grandmother-in-law from his fourth marriage."

"Oh," he said. "But you've heard her talk about the Christmas she worked at Woolworth's before, right?"

"Yes. Every Christmas," I said, wondering what this was leading up to. He was a med student. He was probably going to tell me repeating the same story over and over was a symptom of dementia. Which wouldn't exactly surprise me.

"Is the story consistent?" he asked. "Or does it change from telling to telling?"

"No," I said. "I mean, she tells different details each time, but the story stays basically the same."

"Good," he murmured as if to himself. "And it's a true story? She really *did* work at Woolworth's?"

"As far as I know. I mean, obviously I wasn't there, but she's been telling the story for as long as I've known her. And why would she make up a story about working at *Woolworth's* when she could just as easily have invented one about spending Christmas in Paris or something?"

"That's true," he conceded. "Is there a point to the story? A moral?"

"You mean is it a lecture in disguise, like Aunt Mildred's stories? Things were better in the old days or young people nowadays don't know the meaning of the word 'work' or something? No."

"Hmm, interesting," he said, "but that's not what I meant. I meant is the story about an event in her life, like how she met her husband?"

"No, it's totally pointless."

He frowned for a minute and then said, "Do lots of things remind her of it?"

"Are you kidding? *Everything* reminds her of it."

He nodded as if that was what he'd thought. "Do you know if something traumatic happened while she was working there?"

"Traumatic?" I said blankly.

"Anything shocking or frightening or tragic. Like finding out her boyfriend had been killed in World War II or something."

"I don't think Grandma Elving's quite that old," I said. "Why do you think something happened to her when she worked there?"

"Because memories like hers are triggered by a trauma of some kind."

I was about to ask him what he meant by "memories like hers" when Jillian opened the door, looked daggers at me, like I'd enticed Lassiter in there or something, and said brightly, "Oh, here you are, Lassiter. Sloane, he's in here!" She turned to me. "Good, you're still here, Ori. I was afraid you'd left. You need to take Grandma Elving home."

But at least Part One of the horror was over, and I had four weeks to brace myself for Part Two.

Or not. On Monday morning Grandma Elving called me and asked me if I could give her a ride to an appointment.

"Dave promised he'd drive me," she told me, "but he was called out of town on business, and Sloane's in the mountains, so Jillian said to call you."

Which meant if *I* turned her down, the main topic at Christmas dinner would be how selfish and heartless I was, especially since the appointment turned out to be at a medical clinic in Cherry Creek.

But at least I could make it clear to her that this was a one-time thing. So as soon as I got her in the car, I said, "I'm afraid after today I won't be able to take you places. I've got a job interview this afternoon, and after that I'll be working, but I'd be happy to show you how to call an Uber. They're really fast and reliable."

"So you still haven't found a job for Christmas vacation?" she asked.

"No," I said, and half-expected her to suggest I apply at Woolworth's, even though the store had been out of business for years, but she didn't.

She said, "How would you like a job driving me?" and named an hourly wage that was more than I could make at Starbucks or the mall.

But it would mean having to listen to her Woolworth's story for a solid month. I wasn't sure I could stand that. "I'm waiting to hear about a job at Starbucks," I lied, "and I told them I was available, so…"

"Well, if it doesn't work out, I'd love to have you as my chauffeur. I know how hard it is for students to find a job. That Christmas I worked at Woolworth's, I applied at I don't know how many places before they hired me," and launched into the familiar story of her working at Woolworth's.

"It was so exciting being there. The store was all decorated and the tree by the front door had bubble lights on it. You probably don't know what those are. They were Christmas tree lights shaped like candles, with red and green and gold liquid in them that bubbled when they got hot. They were so pretty."

There was certainly nothing traumatic about that. She sounded happy recounting the story, and her wrinkled face lit up with pleasure at the memory. There was no moral, either, no lectures about what a hard worker she'd been or how girls in her day had known what Christmas really meant.

Which was strange, now that I thought about it. Aunt Mildred wasn't the only old person who told stories about the failings of the younger generation and the vast superiority of the "good old days." Everybody I knew over the age of sixty did. But not Grandma Elving. The fact that the memory was so clear was strange, too. I couldn't remember that many details about Thanksgiving dinner, and that had only been a few days ago.

She was still talking about the Christmas decorations. "They had evergreen garlands strung above the center aisle," she said. "With a big red bow in the center."

"Those are pretty gloves you're wearing," I said. "They look warm."

"Kidskin," she said. "That Christmas I worked at Woolworth's one of the departments I worked in was Leather Goods, and they sold gloves just like these."

Of course they did, I thought. "There's a lot of traffic today," I said, but it didn't even put a dent in the flow.

"They sold all kinds of leather gloves—pigskin and moroccan leather and suede," she said. "And handbags and wallets. And music boxes. Pink and blue ones with satin linings that played 'The Blue Danube' when you opened the lid. Every time I hear that song, I think of those music boxes. Some of them had a little ballerina that spun around, too."

The music boxes got us all the way out Speer. "What street's the doctor's office on?" I asked her.

"Oh, my, I don't know," she said, which surprised me. I'd assumed she was going to see her regular doctor. She must be going to see a specialist.

"I wrote it down," she said, fumbling in her handbag.

And please don't let that remind her of the handbags she used to sell at Woolworth's, I thought.

"Here it is," she said, pulling out a slip of paper.

She read me the address, and I drove to it, wondering what sort of specialist she was going to. The building didn't offer any clue. It listed dozens of clincs and labs, and the door of the office she headed for said only "UCHealth" and under that, "Hayden Clinic."

Grandma Elving gave her name to the receptionist, and she said, "Oh, yes, he's expecting you," and disappeared through a door. I glanced over at the magazine rack, thinking it might have pamphlets that would give me a clue—"Managing Your Cancer" or "The Ten Warning Signs of Heart Disease" or something—but all they had was copies of *Travel* and *People*. No help there. I'd have to hope the doctor, when he came out, would have his specialty on the name-tag of his lab coat.

It didn't. He wasn't wearing a lab coat. He was wearing the same blazer and chinos he'd worn at Thanksgiving dinner. "Lassiter," I said, surprised, "what are you doing here? I thought you were in Vail with Sloane."

"I was. Sloane's still up there. She's staying till Christmas, but I couldn't take that much time off. I've got this research project that's due."

Well, he definitely won't be at Christmas dinner, I thought. Sloane didn't like guys who weren't constantly at her beck and call. "Research project?" I inquired.

"He means me," Grandma Elving said, and when I looked blankly at her, "I'm the project. This young man is going to record my memories of that Christmas I worked at Woolworth's."

"You *are?*" I said.

"Yes," Lassiter said happily. "She's agreed to let me take down a full account of her memory," and I thought, *Oh, you have no idea of what you're letting yourself in for.*

"Are you ready?" Lassiter asked Grandma Elving.

"Yes!" she said.

"Good," Lassiter said, and a nurse appeared at his side. "Anne here is going to get some information from you and have you sign a release form saying that we can use what you say to us during the interview, and then we'll get started."

"Oh, good, I have so much to tell you," Grandma Elving said, and went off with the nurse, and as soon as the door shut behind them, I said, "You want Grandma Elving to tell you about that Christmas she worked at Woolworth's? *Why?*"

"I think Sloane told you on Thanksgiving that I'm working on a project concerning memory. It involves TFBMs, and Mrs. Elving's Woolworth's memory has all the earmarks of being a textbook example."

"TFBMs?"

"Yes, they're memories that are indelible due to the heightened emotional state at the time of the event, like people's memories of the *Challenger* explosion or 9-11. The subject remembers every aspect of the event as if it had been captured on film down to the last detail—sights, sounds, smells, emotions, everything—as if it had just happened. They used to call them flashbulb memories—that's what TFBM stands for, traumatic flashbulb memory—because of the way a flashbulb lit up everything for a blinding instant and then left an after-image, though nowadays no one knows what a flashbulb is. They're marked by being exceptionally vivid, multisensory, and highly detailed."

Well, that definitely describes Grandma Elving's, I thought.

"They're also persistent," Lassiter said. "Unlike ordinary autobiographical memories, which fade over time, TFBMs remain just as

vivid as when they happened for years, sometimes even for a lifetime. It's as if they were
branded into the brain."

And that was definitely Grandma Elving's. But
there must be lots of people who'd had flashbulb
memories that were a lot less boring than hers.
"I still don't understood why you want Grandma
Elving as a subject," I said.

"Because ordinarily we're limited to, one,
asking people with shared TFBMs like I told you
about—the Twin Towers or the *Challenger*—or,
two, interviewing patients suffering from PTSD.
Or, three, simulating TFBMs in the lab in subjects
by having them view, say, a slasher movie, which
is what we've been doing on this project. But all
three methods have drawbacks. Lab-simulated
TFBMs are shallower and last a shorter time than
real memories, and many of them aren't authen-
tic TFBMs at all. And with the ones caused by
an event, you're limited to third-hand data, rely-
ing on transcripts of interviews taken at the time
of the event or else you have to wait for another
event to occur. You can't just produce them to fit
your timetable."

"Unless you're a terrorist," I said.

"Right," Lassiter said. "But blowing things up to produce a memory is frowned on by the medical profession." He grinned.

"What about the PTSD patients?" I asked.

"Calling up their memories can produce anxiety, depression, and even flashbacks. Plus, they're understandably reluctant to revisit the experience that caused the memory, whereas Mrs. Elving is eager to share her story. She's an ideal subject, if her memory's a TFBM. I want to run a battery of tests on her to determine that, but—"

"Hang on," I said. "Tests?" Grandma Elving was eighty, and my stepdad Dave would never forgive me if I let anything happen to her. "What kind of tests? You're not going to stick electrodes in her brain or anything, are you?"

"No, of course not. Nothing invasive," Lassiter assured me. "A questionnaire and a series of targeted questions and then a CT-LLI scan to determine her brain activity as she's remembering the event."

"A CT-what?"

"CT-LLI. Computerized tomographic lattice light-sheet imaging. It's a new kind of scan which combines two technologies to measure neural activity in real time. But before I do the scan I need to get a complete account of the memory from her to determine its parameters and establish a baseline for targeted questioning."

Knowing Grandma Elving, that would take days. Or weeks. I gathered up my scarf and gloves. "What time should I come back and pick her up?"

"Actually, I was hoping you could stay and sit in on the interview," he said. "That is, if you can spare the time," and gave me a smile that made it impossible for me to say no. "I'd like to have you there just in case she needs prompting."

She didn't. After a couple of preliminary questions about which Woolworth's she'd worked at and how old she'd been, she took off and talked for three hours straight, at which point Lassiter's recorder ran out of space, and we had to stop so he could upload the transcript to his computer.

"I told you," I whispered to him when his assistant took Grandma Elving out to show her where the bathroom was. "Are you sorry you did this?"

"No," he said excitedly. "This is exactly what I hoped for. The clarity, the heightened emotional state, the irrelevant details..."

"If it's irrelevant details you want, Grandma Elving's your girl, all right," I said.

"I *know*," he said, completely missing my sarcasm. "Irrelevant details are one of the primary indicators of a TFBM. With ordinary memories, the brain filters out any details that aren't pertinent to the main memory—with a birthday, for instance, you remember the cake and your presents, but not what shoes your mother was wearing or what you had for breakfast that day—but with TFBMs, every bit of detail that was recorded at the moment of the triggering, the moment the metaphorical flashbulb went off, becomes part of the memory."

I thought of the traffic lights and the music boxes.

"There's no filtering," Lassiter said, "so the more irrelevant details she remembers, the more likely it is to be a TFBM, and she's remembered a lot."

"And she still hasn't told you about the bell-ringing Santa Claus and the nativity figures," I said.

"Nativity figures?" he asked, instantly interested.

"You know, like in a nativity scene. Mary and Joseph and the wise men and everything. There were fifteen of them, which is how many times I've heard her talk about them. Listen, when Grandma Elving comes back, I think I'd better take her to get something to eat. It's nearly one o'clock, and she's an old lady."

"You're right," he said. "I wasn't thinking, I was just so excited at the prospect of this being a TFBM. We can finish this up tomorrow."

But Grandma Elving refused to quit or even stop to eat something. "Why doesn't Ori go out and get us sandwiches or whatever it is you young people eat these days and we can eat while we work? That is, if Ori wouldn't mind."

"I'd be glad to," I said. I asked Lassiter what he wanted to eat, got directions to the closest Wendy's, and ducked out just as Grandma Elving started in on the nativity figures.

At least I won't have to listen to that for the sixteenth time, I thought, but when I got back, she was still regaling Lassiter with them.

"We got paid once a week on Fridays," she was saying. "They paid us in cash, and as soon as I picked up my pay packet, I'd go straight down to Christmas Decorations and buy some of them. The first week I bought Mary and Joseph and the baby in the manger, and the next I bought the shepherds."

You're the one who wanted irrelevant details, I thought, handing Lassiter his hamburger and coke, but he looked totally engrossed.

"There were two of them, one kneeling down and one standing up, with a lamb on his shoulders—"

I handed her her tea, but she kept right on talking. "And the third week I bought the sheep— they were only fifteen cents apiece—and the angel and then two of the wise men, and the last week I bought the third one and the camel."

It took her another half hour to get through the nativity set— "You could buy a stable, too, but they were really expensive, and without it, I could arrange the figures so the shepherds were out in the fields and the wise men were in the East, looking up and seeing the star for the first time, realizing what it meant and having a—what's the word I'm looking for? Where you have a sudden flash of insight?"

"Epiphany?" I suggested.

"That's it, having an epiphany," she said. "I thought that was much better than having them all crammed together inside a tiny stable—" and then she moved on to the rest of the things in the Christmas Decorations department, the ornaments and packets of tinsel and bubble lights (which she described all over again) and then onto Toyland, which was in the next aisle over.

"They had Flexible Flyer sleds and Lincoln Logs and talking dolls and a big electric train layout in the middle, with tunnels and bridges and a depot. There were always dozens of children gathered around, watching it." And on and on. This was the first time I'd heard the whole thing uninterrupted (except for my lunch run) and it was just as boring and pointless as I'd been afraid it would be.

And as interminable. Lassiter's tape recorder ran out two more times before he called a halt to it, and even then Grandma Elving wasn't done. "I still haven't told you about the candy counter," she said. "Or the cosmetics counter."

"You can tell me tomorrow," Lassiter said. "I don't want to tire you out."

"Oh, but I'm not tired—"

"Right now Anne's going to check your vitals again and then I want you to go home and get a good night's sleep."

"I'll go get the car and bring it around to the front door," I said, and went out to the waiting room.

Lassiter followed me, and I expected it was to ask me for help in finding a way to tell Grandma Elving he didn't need her to come back, but the moment the door shut, he said excitedly, "Your grandmother's account has all the earmarks of a TFBM, the intensity, the sensory involvement, the irrelevant details, they're all present. I won't know for certain till I do the brain scans, but I'm convinced it's a TFBM. Can you bring her in at eight tomorrow? I want to finish her preliminary interview and then conduct a second one to determine the consistency of her story."

Over the next week I heard her account of that Christmas she worked at Woolworth's at least five times. Grandma Elving loved every second of it. "My, that was fun!" she said when I was driving her home after the third day. "Wasn't it, Ori?"

"Yes," I said, and I wasn't lying, in spite of having to hear her story over and over. The more she rambled on, the more time I got to spend with Lassiter, who was even nicer than I'd thought he was that first night at dinner. And

Grandma Elving was paying me not only for my driving but for the time I spent with her at the lab, so I didn't have to worry about finding another job. And it was more fun than working at the mall would have been. Or Woolworth's in 1960, even though Grandma Elving made it sound like it had been an unmitigated delight from beginning to end.

I'd had Christmas jobs before, so I very much doubted that, and so did Lassiter. He'd had her recount her memory while undergoing an CT-LLI scan, and decided it was definitely a TFBM. "There's activation of the amygdala, the hippocampus, and the pre-frontal cortex. It matches the neural pattern of a TFBM exactly, which means it must have been triggered by some kind of trauma."

"But her memory of that Christmas is so positive. I've never heard her mention anything bad. Couldn't something happy have caused it instead?"

He shook his head. "Happiness isn't a strong enough or a concentrated enough emotion to trigger a TFBM. It's too diffuse. And besides, it has a completely different neural signature. Positive emotions activate the limbic cortex and the precuneus, not the amygdala or the hippocampus."

"But you've heard her," I said. *And heard her and heard her and heard her.* "She's never said a word about a trauma."

"She may not consciously remember it," Lassiter said. "It's common with TFBMs for the core trauma to be repressed and only come out after questioning."

"But wouldn't there be some indication—?"

"There is. The persistence of Mrs. Elving's memory over the years, for one, and her compulsive need to repeat it."

She definitely had that. Even though she spent all day every day talking about it, that wasn't enough. She brought it up at every possible opportunity on our trips to and from the clinic. And when she couldn't find one, she manufactured one. The night before on the way home, she'd said suddenly, apropos of nothing, "The first week I was at Woolworth's, I worked at the cosmetic counter for three days, selling nail polish and Tangee lipsticks and 'Midnight in Paris' perfume. It came in this dark blue bottle, which I thought was the height of sophistication."

But except for the scent of the "Midnight in Paris," which was apparently nauseating and extremely strong, nothing she shared with me was negative, and Lassiter's questioning didn't turn up anything.

When he asked her if she remembered anything negative about her time at Woolworth's, she said, "The customers complained about the prices and having to wait in line, and they were sometimes ill-tempered, like Aunt Mildred. Or condescending like Jillian. Oh, and Mr. Gipson used to yell at Alice and me—"

"Alice?"

"She was another Christmas break hiree. We worked together in Leather Goods and Giftwrapping, and Mr. Gipson would yell at us for giggling and talking when we should have been waiting on customers."

But crabby customers and being dressed down by the boss hardly qualified as traumas, and the personal-history survey Lassiter had her fill out didn't turn up anything either. She hadn't met her husband till the year after she graduated from college, and there hadn't been any family crises, health scares, or deaths during the relevant period, not even the loss of a family pet.

"Could she have found out some terrible family secret?" Lassiter asked me.

"You mean like the knowledge that she was going to be stuck going to horrible holiday dinners for the rest of her life?"

He grinned. "No, I'm serious. What about a car accident in which she was to blame?"

"She didn't have a car," I said. "She took the bus to work, remember? Why don't you just ask her whether something bad happened to her and what it was?"

He shook his head. "That might drive the memory of the trauma even deeper. It must have been something at work," he said thoughtfully. "Maybe she was groped by one of the men she worked with or had an affair with one of them and he got her pregnant—"

Or she fell in love with him, and he didn't even know she was alive, I thought. *Like me.*

"Or she might have shoplifted merchandise or taken money from the cash register," Lassiter went on.

"Grandma *Elving?*" I said. "No. Absolutely not."

"You're right," he said. "And guilt activates a different area of the frontal cortex." He thought a moment. "Maybe it was a shared trauma. When was President Kennedy assassinated?"

"Not till 1963, and the year she worked at Woolworth's was 1960." I looked the year up on my phone. "The Civil Rights Movement started that year, and *Ben Hur* came out," I said, scrolling down through the list of events. "Russia's downing of the U-2 plane, whatever that was... the Vietnam War—"

"There you go. She fell in love with someone she met at Woolworth's that Christmas and he was killed in Vietnam."

"But the war had hardly started," I said, looking it up on my phone. "The draft didn't begin till 1969."

"Then that's probably not it," Lassiter said. "But there has to be something."

But successive sessions failed to turn anything up (except more irrelevant details—the wise men had been named Caspar, Melchior, and Balthazar, the lunch counter had sold hot dogs and hamburgers as well as ice cream sodas) and Lassiter grew more and more frustrated. "I know there's a trauma in there," he told me. "I want to do another CT-LLI, only this time with memory enhancement. There's a new experimental drug, Reminizil. It recreates the original intensity of the TFBM."

"I thought you said you weren't going to do anything invasive."

"This isn't. It's perfectly safe. No harmful side effects."

"How do you know that? You said it was experimental. Some side effects take months to show up, and Grandma Elving's eighty and awfully frail."

She was also awfully determined. When I tried to talk her out of taking the drug, she told me, "I'm doing it. I've already signed the permission forms. You're as bad as Dave, so over-protective. I'll be fine," and I had to comfort myself with the knowledge (gleaned from the internet) that the clinical trials of Reminizil had shown only minor side effects—headaches and fatigue—though I was still worried.

And so, it turned out, was Grandma Elving, though not for the reasons I expected. At the last minute, after the nurse had put in the IV and was about to start the feed for the Reminizil, Grandma Elving asked Lassiter, "This isn't like truth serum, is it? Where you take it and tell the doctor everything you're thinking?"

"You mean like sodium pentathol?" he said. "No. All it will do is help you remember."

"And the scan thing won't show what I'm thinking?"

"No."

"Look, Grandma Elving," I said, "if you don't want to do this, you don't have to."

"No, no, I want to," she said. "Go ahead and inject the Reminizil."

The nurse did, and Lassiter proceeded with the scan, taking her through her story all over again and watching the shifting images of her brain's activity on the screen.

I was watching the screen that had her pulse and heart rate on it, worried that he'd been wrong, and Reminizil—or the shock of remembering the trauma—might cause a stroke, but nothing happened. And I do mean nothing. If Lassiter had expected Grandma Elving to suddenly say, "Oh, my God, now I remember! Something terrible happened that Christmas!" he was sorely disappointed.

Her answers to Lassiter's questions were just the same, and after the scan, she clasped his hand with her bony, veined one in gratitude. "*Thank* you for giving me the Reminizil. It was just like I was back there, living through it all over again!" she said. "I could hear the cash registers and see the garlands and smell the 'Midnight in Paris'!" and when Lassiter asked her how she felt while she was remembering it, she said, "Wonderful! That was the happiest Christmas of my life."

"Maybe she's telling the truth, and it was," I said to Lassiter while she was being unhooked from the IV.

"No, the activation of the amygdala and the hippocampus were even stronger with the Reminizil. There's definitely a trauma. It's just buried in the subconscious, probably because it's something too painful or too humiliating for her to remember."

"Then should we be dredging it up?" I asked, thinking how happy she'd been talking about Woolworth's and the snow and the bubble lights. "Maybe she'd be better off *not* remembering."

Lassiter shook his head. "She has an obsessive need to retrieve it. That's why she keeps returning to it again and again. She's trying to exorcise the trauma."

I wasn't convinced of that. Her reminiscing didn't strike me as obsessive but as fond, and I kept remembering what he'd said before about how forcing PTSD patients to recall their experiences had caused flashbacks and traumatized them all over again. Maybe it would be better to stop now and let her keep thinking that Christmas had been a happy one.

But when I broached the subject of quitting to her, using the excuse that all the trips to the lab and tests and interview sessions might be wearing her out, she refused to consider it.

"I'm perfectly fine," she said, and looked at me shrewdly. "What's wrong? Has something happened between you and Lassiter?"

"No, of course not."

"Good," she said. "The two of you make such a nice couple."

No, we don't, I thought. *He doesn't even know I exist.*

"But if you're getting along, then why all this talk about my quitting?" Grandma Elving said, looking suspiciously at me. "Did Lassiter tell you my memory isn't the kind he needs for his study?"

"No, of course not," I lied. "Lassiter thinks you're a wonderful subject."

"Good," she said, and started telling me about the dry goods department at Woolworth's, but a few minutes later, she said, "Yesterday I heard Lassiter telling Dr. Riordan my memory was a TFBM. What does that stand for?"

Lassiter had said asking her directly about her trauma would only drive it further underground, but saying I didn't know what TFBM stood for was likely to make her even more suspicious.

"It stands for Traumatic Flashbulb Memory because it lights up the entire event, just like a flashbulb," I said rapidly. "When Lassiter told me, I had to ask him what a flashbulb was. I'd never seen one. Do you know what they are?" I asked, hoping she'd focus on that and forget I'd said "traumatic."

It worked. She said, "We sold them at Woolworth's, at the camera counter, along with camera cases and tripods and film. You probably don't know what film is either. It came in little square yellow boxes with 'Kodachrome' printed in red. The camera counter was next to the pipes and tobacco counter, and next to that was the candy counter," and launched into a description of gumdrops and chocolate creams and ribbon candy.

I was relieved she hadn't picked up on the trauma thing, and even more relieved the next morning when she didn't bring up the TFBMs again. But she didn't bring up anything that might point to a trauma either, and when I went out to fetch lunch, Lassiter followed me down to the car.

"I've been looking at her physical responses during the scan," he said. "None of the stress indicators—pulse rate, muscular tension, skin conduction—showed any elevation."

"So what does that mean? That there isn't a trauma after all?"

"No, I'm absolutely certain the neural signature matches that of a TFBM. But it could mean the trauma's so deeply buried it's undetectable even to her brain's stress centers, which means it's too deeply buried to be retrieved, and without it..."

You can't finish your project, so you're going to have to find someone else for your study, I thought, and spent a good part of the afternoon session listening to Grandma Elving prattle on happily about the stationery department and the Santa Claus on the street outside and the lunch counter, thinking about how impossible it was going to be to find another Christmas job at this late date and how much I was going to miss Lassiter.

"I was terrible at working at the lunch counter," Grandma Elving said. "I couldn't get the hang of the malted milk machine. I kept spewing ice cream everywhere, so they assigned me to doing balloons."

"Balloons?" I said. "At Christmas?"

"Yes, they had these red and green balloons taped to the mirror behind the lunch counter, each with a slip of paper inside with a price on it: ten cents, twenty-five cents, all the way up to a dollar, and the customer picked a balloon and we popped it for them, and that was the price the customer paid for Woolworth's special Candy Cane Sundae. My job was to write out the slips of paper and stick them in the balloons and then blow up the balloons and tie them, but they kept getting away from me and flying all over the store…" She stopped, an odd, bemused expression on her face.

"What is it?" Lassiter asked. She had put her hand to her forehead as if it hurt.

"What's wrong?" I asked. "Grandma Elving?"

"Nothing," she said. "It's just…for a moment there I thought I remembered something."

"What was it?" Lassiter asked eagerly.

"I don't know. You know how when there's a word on the tip of your tongue, but you can't think of it. It was like that. Only it wasn't a word. It was…" Her voice trailed off.

"It was what?" Lassiter prompted. "Did it have something to do with the balloons? Or the lunch counter?"

"No, I don't think so," she said, frowning. "I don't know *what* it was," and no matter how many questions Lassiter asked her, the memory didn't return.

"I'm sorry," Grandma Elving said as we left for the day. "Whatever it was, it's gone."

But Lassiter was still elated. "The memory of the trauma's starting to break through," he'd told me just before we left.

He was right. While I was driving her home, she stopped in the middle of telling me about buying one of the wise men for her nativity set and stared blankly at the windshield for a minute before exclaiming, "Drat! I almost had it!"

And the next day, answering a question about who all she'd worked with at Woolworth's, she said, "There was Mr. Gipson and Mrs. Solomon— she worked at the candy counter—and Alice. We worked in Gloves and Scarves together..." She ticked the names off on her fingers as she said them. "And Tom at the lunch counter, and Marty..."

She paused, and Lassiter looked up alertly. "What is it? Did you remember something?"

"Ye-e-s," she said doubtfully. "I'm not sure. This is so annoying, not to be able to remember. You don't think it's a sign of Alzheimer's, do you?"

"No, not at all," Lassiter said. "It's perfectly normal. Now, you were telling me about the people who worked at the lunch counter—"

"Oh, yes," she said. "There were Tom and Marty and another boy named Ralph, he had this mass of curly hair, and Mr. Gipson made him wear a hairnet like the girls." She laughed. "Oh, and speaking of hairnets, there was Mrs. Proudy. She worked in Leather Goods, and she wore a hairnet, too, and those thick brown cotton stockings." Which led to a story about the nylons they'd sold "in little flat boxes, layered in tissue paper."

"You told us Woolworth's sold a special Christmas sundae?" Lassiter asked, obviously trying to get her back to the lunch counter and Marty.

"Oh, yes, the Candy Cane Sundae," she said. "It was made with peppermint ice cream and hot fudge sauce and whipped cream, with crushed green and red peppermint candy on top and a candy cane stuck in the side."

"And who made those? Marty?"

"Marty," she said. "You never see green candy canes anymore, just red. You never see those pastel

mints we used to sell, either, the round ones, pale green and yellow and pink. Woolworth's used to sell them in boxes, to husbands mainly, looking for a last-minute gift for their wives. They'd come in right before Christmas, looking desperately for something, anything to buy. Like a can opener. When I worked in Kitchenwares, they'd do that all the time. Not an electric can opener—they didn't sell those at Woolworth's—just an ordinary hand-crank one."

"Going back to the sundaes, you said Marty was in charge of making them," Lassiter persisted. "Did you help him?"

"No," she said. "I mean, can you imagine someone giving their wife a can opener for Christmas? I'd suggest a box of the pastel mints or something up in Cosmetics, bath powder or a bottle of 'Midnight in Paris' or an assortment of bubble bath or something," she said, and veered off into how the bubble bath had come in little paper packets, "like the ones seeds come in, with a picture of flowers on the front—rose or lilies-of-the-valley or jasmine."

The message was clear. She didn't want to talk about Marty.

"The trauma definitely has something to do with him," Lassiter told me. "Maybe he took her into the back room and—what did they call it back then?—deflowered her?"

"Exactly how old do you think she is?"

"Sorry," he said. "But back then, lots of nineteen-year-olds were virgins, weren't they? And if he dumped her afterwards and went off with some other employee…"

He was right. If she'd had sex with Marty and then caught him with Alice who she'd worked in Gloves and Scarves with, that could have been the kind of thunderbolt moment that could produce a TFBM. And there'd almost certainly been date rape back then, too. But I hadn't heard any fear or revulsion in her voice at all when she mentioned Marty.

But the memory definitely involved Marty. The next day, in the middle of Lassiter's asking her about the nativity figures, she suddenly said, "Oh! I just remembered something. You know those balloons I told you about? Well, I was trying to tie a knot in the end of one of them, and I lost hold of it, and it went whizzing all over the store and knocked over a whole display of Old Spice and Aqua Velva aftershaves in Cosmetics, and Marty said, 'They should put you in charge of the missile program. You're deadly.' It was so funny."

"And is that the thing you've been trying to remember?"

"No," she said, frowning. "But it's connected somehow..."

"To Marty?" Lassiter asked. "Or the lunch counter?"

"I don't know." She smiled apologetically. "I'm sorry I'm having so much trouble remembering it."

"That's okay," Lassiter said. "These things take time," but time was just what we didn't have. His project was due at the beginning of January, and Christmas was coming up fast, which meant he only had two weeks left, and at this rate it would take months to worm the trauma out of her.

She must have been thinking along the same lines, because the next morning she said, "I had an idea. What if we went to the store?"

"You mean the Woolworth's where you worked?" Lassiter said.

"It's not there, Grandma Elving," I said. "It closed years ago."

"I *know* that. But last night I got to thinking, maybe seeing the building where it used to be might help me remember."

Not if it's a trauma you're deliberately trying to forget, I said to myself, but Lassiter thought it was worth trying.

"Memory's frequently context-dependent," he said. "Visiting the—" He stopped, and it was obvious he'd intended to say, "the scene of the crime." "Visiting the site of the original memory might trigger it," he said instead.

"But it's so far for you to walk," I objected. "Driving's not allowed on Sixteenth Street, and parking downtown is a nightmare. Plus, it's so raw and windy out. You might catch cold."

"Nonsense," she said. "I'm a tough old bird."

The only thing birdlike about her was the lightness and brittleness of her bones, but she refused to be talked out of it, and the next day Lassiter and I found ourselves driving her downtown, bundling her into a wheelchair, tucking a wool blanket around her, and wheeling her over to the corner of Sixteenth and Champa where her Woolworth's had been.

It was now a 7-Eleven with loft apartments above it, and across the street were a Planet Fitness and a Thai restaurant which obviously hadn't been there the Christmas she'd worked there.

"That was the corner where I caught the bus," she said, pointing at the restaurant. "There was a newsstand there, and next to it a cigar store. And in front of it was where the Santa Claus stood with his black kettle, ringing his bell. I can remember coming out of the front door after work—it was dark by then—and seeing him ringing his bell in the snow. It snowed nearly every day. And I remember the Christmas lights. They were strung above the street, with wreaths in the middle, and when the wind blew they would swing back and forth, like bells tolling."

The wind was definitely blowing today, a biting wind that whipped icily around the corners, but Grandma Elving didn't seem to notice, she was so busy remembering what stores had once been there. "There was a shoe repair shop there," she said, pointing at the Planet Fitness gym. "It had a neon sign that said, 'Soles While You Wait.' With a 'U' instead of the word 'You.' It was right next to a Christian Science reading room, and I always thought the sign should be in their window instead."

"What about the store?" Lassiter said, turning her wheelchair so she was facing the building where the Woolworth's had been. "Do you remember where the door was?'

"Yes, it was right there," she said, pointing at one of the windows of the 7-Eleven. "It was a big double door, and above it was the store's name in gold letters on a red background— F.W. Woolworth & Co.—and in the corners, 5c and 10c," and looked like she was seeing it right now.

And seeing the whole store. "The candy counter was near the door," she said, pointing, "and so was Christmas merchandise—tinned fruitcakes and bath sets and shaving mugs, and over in the corner was Giftwrapping. I loved working in Giftwrapping because you could see outside, the cars and the people hurrying by with their shopping bags and packages, all bundled up in their hats and scarves and boots."

"Where would the lunch counter have been?" Lassiter asked.

"There," she said, pointing to the left. "It stretched half the length of the store. It had stools all along it and booths coming out from it, like that," she said, gesturing.

"And you and Marty and Ralph worked behind the counter?"

"Yes, I made the sandwiches and dished up the blue plate specials and the boys grilled the hamburgers and hot dogs and made the fountain drinks, which was good. The first cherry coke I tried to make, I got cherry syrup all over, and Marty said—"

She stopped short. "The cosmetics and notions departments were in the middle," she said, starting again, "and over there," she pointed to the right, "was Gloves and Scarves, and behind it was Stationery, which I loved working in because Andy worked there. He was so cute."

"Before when you were telling us about the lunch counter and Marty," Lassiter said, kneeling down next to her wheelchair, "did you remember something?"

"No," she said, but doubtfully, and then burst out, "It's so maddening! Every time I think I have it, it disappears!"

"It's okay," he said. "Do you want to go look at the side of the building?"

"Yes," she said, and he wheeled her down the side of the building and back and then down Sixteenth Street, where she'd walked during her lunch hour to look at the decorated Christmas windows.

"Neusteter's windows had Santa's Workshop in them," she said, pointing at the shops as we passed, "with elves making toys and Mrs. Claus taking cookies out of the oven, and the Denver Dry had the Nutcracker." Her teeth chattered as she talked, and she was beginning to shiver.

"We need to get her home," I told Lassiter. "She shouldn't be out in this cold," and he nodded.

"Oh, do we have to go?" Grandma Elving said. "Isn't there a lunch counter around here where we can get a cup of coffee and warm up?"

"I think the last lunch counter closed around the same time Woolworth's did," Lassiter said.

"And you're going to catch cold if you stay out in this," I said, starting down the street toward the car.

"But I was just starting to remember things," she said. "Surely there's somewhere we could go."

"There's probably a Starbucks somewhere," Lassiter said, looking vaguely around.

There was, a block up on Sixteenth. I found it on my phone. "Oh, good," Grandma Elving said. "I've always wanted to see what Starbucks was like. I've heard so much about them. And they'll be all decorated for Christmas," and

Lassiter obligingly wheeled her up the sidewalk to it and inside.

"Oh, my," she said, looking around at the metal-and-glass décor and the minimalist blond furniture. "It's so…plain."

"Not like Woolworth's?" Lassiter said.

"*No*," she said emphatically, and it was clear she didn't approve of Starbucks' lack of holiday decorations. The only concessions they'd made to the holidays were a few random white snowflakes stuck on the walls, and green cups embossed with the word "JOY!" in block letters, and I could imagine how different it must look from the crowded, bustling variety store she remembered, with its cluttered aisles and riot of colors and scents and sounds, its jangling cash registers and music.

There was piped-in music here, too, but it was a muted jazz rendition of "Santa Baby," and there was nothing on the blond shelves but brown-foil bags of coffee beans and metal to-go cups.

Grandma Elving looked even more disapproving when she found out she couldn't order a plain cup of coffee. "They have different blends of coffee," Lassiter explained, "and you have to specify whether you want a flat white or a cappuccino or an americano."

"They have peppermint lattes," I put in. "That's a little like Woolworth's candy cane sundae. How about that?"

She consented, and Lassiter went over to order while I helped her out of her coat. "So is this where young people go on dates these days?" she asked, looking at a couple over in the corner.

"Yes, sometimes," I said, piling her coat on an empty chair.

"I can see why," she mused. "It would be a good place to sit and talk and get to know each other. Not like Woolworth's. It was so noisy, and employees only got half an hour for lunch, barely time enough to eat, let alone talk."

"Did you eat at the lunch counter?" I asked her, wondering if that was when she might have talked to Marty and gotten to know him.

"Sometimes," she said. "We got a fifteen percent discount. Or I brought my lunch or didn't eat lunch at all. I just bought a bag of roasted nuts and ate them while I took a walk down Sixteenth and looked at the people and the windows."

Lassiter came back with the lattes and slices of frosted gingerbread, which set Grandma Elving off on a long description of the tins of ginger snaps

Woolworth's had sold, after which she asked if Starbucks had a restroom.

I had to explain that you had to ask at the counter for the code and then had to punch it in, which made her look even more disapproving, so I went with her and punched the code in for her. "Do you want me to wait here for you?" I asked her.

"No, of course not. Go talk to Lassiter."

I came back and sat down next to him. He was poring over the notes he'd taken while we were outside Woolworth's. "This guy Marty obviously had something to do with it," he said. "And the lunch counter."

"And the nativity figures she bought," I added.

"Right." He jotted that down. "Can you think of anything else?"

"The snow," I suggested, gazing around at the Starbucks, with its stark, cheerless décor and bare plate-glass windows. It wasn't very Christmasy compared to the bright, bustling scene Grandma Elving had described, but it was still nice. I wished I could go on sitting there in the darkening afternoon with Lassiter, our heads together over his notes, forever.

Which reminded me, Grandma Elving had been in the bathroom an awfully long time. I hoped she was all right. That wind had been so icy. I hoped she hadn't gotten hypothermia or something. "I think I'd better go check on her," I said, but before I could stand up, she came out.

She had an odd look on her face. "Are you all right?" I asked anxiously.

"Yes. While I was washing my hands, I remembered something. You know the Civic Center and how they light it up at Christmas? I think we should go see it."

"Tonight?" I said. "I don't think that's a good idea. It's too cold."

"Why do you want to go see it?" Lassiter asked. "Did you think the Civic Center has something to do with the thing you can't remember?"

"I'm not sure," she said. "The bus I took home after work went right by it, and I always tried to sit on the right side so I could see it. The lights were so beautiful, all different colors. They had a nativity scene with figures just like the ones I bought every week, only life-sized, and I had the feeling, standing there washing my hands, that if I could just see them, it might bring back the thing that keeps eluding me."

"Really?" Lassiter said eagerly, and I thought disloyally, *No, not really. She just wants to go see the lights. And she doesn't want to go home. She wants the day to keep going, just like I do,* and as I thought it, I suddenly had the same feeling Grandma Elving had just described, that there was something important in what I'd just thought, something that held the key to this whole TFBM thing but was just beyond my grasp. I shook my head like she had, trying to think what it was.

"We can definitely take you to Civic Center to see the lights," Lassiter was saying.

"*No,*" I said. "I think we should take you home, Grandma Elving. You've already put in a long day, and it's miles to the car—"

"You two can stay here while I go get it," Lassiter said. "I can pick you up right out front."

"And we don't have to get out," Grandma Elving added. "We could just drive past. Lassiter's car has a really good heater."

I knew when I was beaten.

But it didn't take a few minutes to drive past. There was an endless line of cars "just driving past" and stopping to see the colors projected on the steps and pillars of the huge curved building turn from purple to blue to red and then green, and there were so many people walking in and around the displays we couldn't even see the nativity scene. We ended up having to get out and push Grandma Elving's wheelchair up to it.

But I'd been wrong about her just stalling. When we reached the nativity scene, sandwiched between a menorah and a giant Frosty the Snowman, she looked for a long moment at the wise men standing by the manger with their gifts and then said softly, "*I* didn't buy the Caspar and Melchior. Marty did."

"Marty from the lunch counter?" Lassiter asked.

"Yes," she said. "I told him I didn't have enough money to buy all three because I still had to buy the shepherds and the donkey, and he said, 'I'll buy them for you.' How could I have forgotten that?"

"Do you remember what happened next?" Lassiter asked.

"Yes," she said, staring at the turbaned Magi. "I said, 'You don't have to do that,' and he said…" Her voice trailed off.

"He said—?" Lassiter prompted.

"I'm freezing," Grandma Elving said, and she looked it. Her thin, wrinkled face was pinched and drawn. "You were right, Ori, this wind is too cold to be out in. I think we'd better go back to the car."

"Of course," Lassiter said. "Let's get you home."

But we didn't take her home. By the time we'd reached the car, Grandma Elving had recovered her color and her spirits and was asking Lassiter if he knew a good restaurant nearby. "I want to take you two out to dinner to thank you for hauling me around all day," and over pasta, she said, "The nativity figures definitely are the key to my remembering. I think if—"

"We are *not* taking you back to the Civic Center," I said.

"No, no, I'm talking about the nativity figures I bought. If I could see them, I'm certain I could remember."

"Do you still have them?"

"No. I kept them on my mantelpiece—I always put them up on the Friday before Christmas because that was when I bought the last one—but they got lost when I moved to the retirement community. Although I've always suspected Jillian threw them out. She and Dave helped me move, you know, and she always turned up her nose at them. She thought they were cheap-looking. But I was thinking, maybe it would be possible to find some in an antique store…"

"No," I said. The last thing Grandma Elving needed was to spend hours on her feet looking for plaster wise men, and most antique stores had aisles too narrow for a wheelchair. And in spite of her protestations, I was still worried about the effect the cold air had had on her. "One long day running around downtown is tiring enough. You—"

"I didn't mean *me*," she said. "I meant the two of you could look *for* me. I could describe them to you so you could go see if you could find them," and that was just what she did—Mary in a pink robe, blue cape, white shawl; Joseph with brown hair, a beard, and a brown robe, and lavender coat; Balthazar in a turban and red robe, etc.—and Lassiter and I spent the next day at his apartment looking on the internet for them.

EBay didn't have any that matched her description, and neither did Etsy, and all the ones for sale on other sites were far too fancy, done in porcelain and carved teak and jade. "I guess it's going to have to be antique stores," Lassiter said, and for the two days after that we searched through them and religious supply houses and gift shops, where we found all kinds of nativity sets, from ones with snowmen as Mary and Joseph and the shepherds to ones with teddy bears, cats, figures made of Legos, and rubber duckies.

"Can you believe this?" Lassiter said laughingly holding up a crèche with aliens as the figures and a flying saucer as the star.

"At least it's better than that Mexican Day of the Dead one we saw with the skeleton figures," I said. "And the one with the fish."

"Oh, I kind of liked that one," Lassiter said. "Especially the octopus wise man. And the starfish star. Speaking of fish, I saw a sushi place in the next block. Do you want to go there for lunch?"

Spending time with Lassiter was wonderful, and I was happy Grandma Elving was at home out of the cold and getting some rest, especially since the weather was getting progressively colder, but I felt guilty, too. Fun as it was, our search wasn't getting us anywhere. All we had to show for our efforts was a plaster donkey and a string of bubble lights, neither of which triggered any memories of Marty in Grandma Elving.

"The donkey's too big," she said. "The figures were only this high," and held her hands four inches apart. "Did you try the thrift stores?"

"We'll check there tomorrow," Lassiter said.

"I can do it," I said. "Lassiter needs to work on his project. January's coming up fast. Christmas is next Monday."

"That's true," Grandma Elving said, but early the next morning she called and said, "You need to take me downtown again. I just saw the weather forecast on TV, and it's supposed to snow. I'm sure I'll be able to remember something if I can see Woolworth's while it's snowing. I've already called Lassiter. He said he'd meet us there."

She was right about the snow. It started to fall as I parked the car, coming down in feathery flakes that swirled around us as we pushed her wheelchair up Sixteenth Street to where the store had been. "It looks just like it did back then!" Grandma Elving cried, clapping her gloved hands in delight.

"Are you remembering anything?" Lassiter asked.

"Yes," she said, gazing at the street. "I remember looking out the front door—it was five o'clock and already dark out. I was going home and I was trying to see if the bus was there yet...and I saw it was starting to snow. It was so beautiful…" Her voice trailed off, and I knew she was seeing not the grubby 7-Eleven, out of which a guy with long greasy hair and a shaggy beard was coming, but the busy street as it had been, full of traffic and Christmas shoppers hurrying past, their arms laden with packages and their shoulders hunched against the falling snow. I could almost see her standing there, young and eager, looking happily out at the snow.

"Bing Crosby was singing 'Silver Bells,' about the street lights blinking a bright red and green," she said. "They were, and I stood there in the doorway watching them, as customers pushed past me, coming in out of the snow. The snow came in with them, in little swirling gusts. You could smell it. It had a sharp, wet smell…"

She stopped again, sitting there in her wheel-chair, staring blindly ahead.

Lassiter looked down at her. "Can you—?" he began.

Don't, I thought, and reached out to keep him from talking. He'd only interrupt her remembering. I put a warning hand on his shoulder.

Grandma Elving gave a little cry, like she was in pain.

"What is it?" Lassiter said.

"I just remembered something about Marty." She grabbed my sleeve. "When you put your hand on Lassiter's shoulder just now—"

"*Here* you are," Sloane said, and Lassiter and I both turned around.

She was standing there dressed all in white—white ski parka and pants, white fur-topped boots—like some malevolent angel.

"I've been looking for you all over, Lassiter," she said. "The lab said you were down here, but they didn't say which block."

"I thought you were in Aspen," Lassiter said.

"Obviously," she said, glaring at me. She turned back to Lassiter. "There wasn't any snow—at least not till today. Wouldn't you know it? It snows the minute I leave—so I came back early. Grandma Elving, what on earth is Ori doing taking you out in this weather?"

"I'm working with Lassiter on his memory project," Grandma Elving said.

"I know," Sloane said. "The nurse at the lab told me. Why didn't you tell me about it, Lassiter? I'd have been glad to help. You didn't have to drag Ori into it." She turned to me. "Don't you have a Christmas job you should be at?"

"This *is* her Christmas job," Grandma Elving said. "She's my driver."

"Oh, I can drive you from now on," Sloane said. "You don't need Ori."

"She hasn't just been driving Mrs. Elving," Lassiter began. She's been helping me with—" but it was no use.

"Whatever it is she's been doing, I can do it," Sloane said. "Ori, if you need a ride home, I can call an Uber." She pulled out her phone.

"I want Ori to drive me home," Grandma Elving said.

"I'll take you," Sloane said firmly, "and then you can take me out to lunch, Lassiter, and tell me all about your project. Let me just call Uber—"

"That's not necessary," I said. "I have my car here."

"Oh, good," she said, putting her phone away and tucking her arm through Lassiter's in a clear dismissal. I was surprised she didn't add, "You may go."

"Ori—" Lassiter said.

"No, that's all right, Lassiter," I told him. "You two take Grandma Elving home. She needs to get in out of this snow, and you need to find out what she remembered before she forgets it. I'll go check the thrift stores."

I turned and walked rapidly away. Behind me I heard Sloane say, "I have so much to tell you about Aspen," and Lassiter ask Grandma Elving, "Right before Sloane came you said you remembered something about Marty. What was it?"

"Marty?" she said vaguely.

"You were talking about standing in the door, looking at the snow—"

I didn't hear her answer, but that evening when I called Grandma Elving to make sure she hadn't caught cold, I asked her the same thing, and she said, "Whatever it was, it's gone. If that dreadful Sloane hadn't interrupted me—"

"I know," I said.

I had known all along it was too good to last. I told myself it was a good sign that Sloane was so threatened she was willing to put up with Grandma Elving's Woolworth story, but who was I kidding, and anyway, it didn't matter. What mattered was finding some way to get Grandma Elving to remember so Lassiter could complete his project, Sloane or no Sloane. So I spent two days scrounging through Goodwills and ARCs looking for nativity figures like hers, but without any success.

On the twenty-second Dave called to remind me of Christmas dinner. "Dad," I said, "did you ever hear Grandma Elving mention someone named Marty who worked at Woolworth's with her?"

"Marty?" he said blankly. "No. Why?"

"Did she ever mention anything bad that happened there that Christmas?" I persisted. "Anything upsetting or sad?"

"Sad?" he repeated incredulously. "Are you kidding? It was the happiest time of her life. That's why she talks about it all the time. We're having dinner at six. We'll see you then. Jillian said to tell you Sloane's bringing Lassiter."

Of course she did, I thought. "I'm not sure I can make it," I said, but he'd already hung up.

The twenty-fourth it snowed again, so much the news said to stay off the roads if possible, so I went back to looking online, with no luck, and then googled "Marty December 1960," to see if I could find any record of an accident or a crime involving someone of that name, but it was too far back. The only things I found were an article on a baseball player named Marty Kutyna and some old *Spin and Marty* comic books on sale on eBay.

At eight that night Grandma Elving called. "Hello? Ori?" she said shakily. "Can you come over?"

"What's wrong?" I said. "What's happened? Are you all right?"

"Yes," she said, but she didn't sound like it. "I'm...I can't seem to catch my breath."

She has pneumonia, I thought. I knew I shouldn't have taken her out in that snow. "Do you have a fever? Does your chest hurt?"

"No..." she said uncertainly. "I had some pain..."

"What kind of pain? A sharp pain?" I asked, trying to remember what the symptoms of a heart attack were. "Does your arm hurt?"

"No..." she said. "I just...it's so hard to breathe."

"I'll be right there," I said, already pulling on my coat. "Listen, I want you to call 911—"

"But—"

"I don't know how long it'll take me to get there in this snow, and you don't have any business waiting. Call 911 and tell them you need an ambulance," I said, wishing I could tell her to stay on the line, but then she wouldn't be able to call 911.

"I'll be there as soon as I can," I said. "Call 911," and hung up before she could raise any objections.

I yanked on my boots, grabbed my keys, and ran out to the car. I didn't bother with the scraper. I brushed the snow off the windshield with my hands and took off for her apartment, hoping against hope this wasn't a heart attack. *I should never have let Lassiter give her that Reminizil*, I thought. *I knew there might be side effects.*

The streets were really slick, which meant I couldn't go as fast as I wanted for fear of having an accident, but hopefully it wouldn't matter. The ambulance would have already arrived, and as I turned into her apartment complex, I looked anxiously ahead for its flashing lights.

There weren't any. *They've already taken her to the hospital*, I thought, and then sickeningly, *or they were too late and there's no need for lights or sirens.*

I knocked on the door, but there was no answer. I tried the door. It wasn't locked. I flung it open and ran inside, calling, "Grandma Elving? Grandma Elving?"

She was sitting in an armchair, breathing hard, as if she'd just climbed a flight of stairs. "Oh, good," she said between breaths, "you're here."

I knelt beside her chair. "Are you still having the pain in your chest?"

"It wasn't a pain exactly," she said. "I just can't seem to catch my breath. I wanted to tell you—"

"Not now," I said. "Did you call 911 like I told you to?"

"No."

Of course not. I pulled out my phone, but before I could press the numbers, the door banged open again and Lassiter burst in, asking, "Are you all right, Mrs. Elving?" and me, "Have you called 911?"

"I was doing that right now," I said.

"No," Grandma Elving said, grabbing his arm with surprising energy. "I don't need an ambulance. Can't you take me?"

"Yes, it'll be faster," Lassiter said. "Get her coat."

I wrestled her into it while Lassiter helped her into her boots. "Ready?" he asked her, and she nodded.

"You'll need your ID and Medicare card," I said. "Lassiter, you go ahead and take her. I'll get her purse and catch up with you at the hospital."

"No. You *have* to come with us."

"All right," I said, and to Lassiter, "Get her in the car and I'll get her purse. Is it in the bedroom?"

"*No*," she called after me as he helped her outside, sounding genuinely upset, and I realized this had rattled her more than she'd shown. "It's in the hall closet."

I found her purse, fumbled in it for her keys, locked the apartment door, and got in the back seat. "Call St. Luke's and tell them we're coming," Lassiter said, and took off at top speed in spite of the ice.

I did and then leaned forward to ask Grandma Elving how she was doing. "Better," she said. "I think it may just have been indigestion. I'm not sure you need to—"

"We're taking you to the hospital," I said firmly, and looked to Lassiter for confirmation, but his attention was all on the snow and the icy streets, and he didn't need any distractions, so I resisted the impulse to quiz Grandma

Elving about her symptoms and when they'd started. She'd stopped panting, so that was good, at least.

We rode in silence for several blocks, and then Grandma Elving said, "I really don't think all this fuss is necessary, but since you're here, I wanted to tell you, I finally remembered what it was that came to me the other day."

"You did?" I said, and glanced at Lassiter, but he gave no sign he'd heard her. He was leaning forward trying to see through the curtain of falling snow.

"Yes," she said. "I was thinking about it tonight after supper. I was looking out the window at the snow and thinking about our having gone downtown and what I'd been telling you before Sloane came along and ruined everything, and…" She put her hand to her chest.

"Are you feeling the pain again?" I asked.

"Pain?" she said blankly. "Oh, you mean the pain I had in my chest. No. And it wasn't a pain exactly. It was more a tightness. And it's not important. I'm trying to tell you—"

"We're nearly there," Lassiter said. "That's the hospital up ahead."

"Before we get there," Grandma Elving said, "I need to tell you. I remembered. Your Reminizil worked."

"It worked all right," I said bitterly. "So well it's landed you in the hospital," and when Lassiter turned to meet my gaze in the rearview mirror, "You told me it didn't have any side effects."

"The research—"

"Well, the *research* was obviously wrong," I said as he pulled up in front of the emergency room entrance. "Because here we are. You—" I began, but Grandma Elving cut me off.

"You are *not* to blame Lassiter," she said. "This isn't his fault."

"No, it's mine, because I didn't stop him from giving it to you. I should have—"

"It's not your fault either. Or the Reminizil's. It didn't have anything to do with this."

"You don't know that for sure."

"Yes, I do, and if I'd known you were going to react that way—" she said. "I was *trying* to tell you I'd remembered the thing that's been eluding me these last few weeks—"

Lassiter had stopped in front of the entrance. "You can tell us later," I said, and got out. We helped her out of the car and into the emergency room. They quizzed me briefly on her symptoms and then whisked her into the nether regions of the emergency room while I took care of the paperwork and Lassiter parked the car, and then took us back to a curtained cubicle where a team of nurses were busy hooking her up to an EKG and IVs and taking blood. "Is all this fuss necessary?" she said to them. "I was just a little out of breath."

"And she had chest pains," I said, whereupon they asked her a whole series of questions about her symptoms, to which she gave answers just as vague as the ones she'd given us.

The ER doctor came in and asked the same questions. When Lassiter told her about his project and the Reminizil, she asked, "When was that?" and when Lassiter told her, said, "It would be out of the patient's system by now."

"What about residual side effects?" I asked, and she said, "I'll check," but she didn't seem especially concerned about it, and I felt a little bit reassured.

"We're going to run some tests," she said, and shooed us out to the waiting room.

"Look," Lassiter said earnestly, "if I'd thought the Reminizil would result in any harmful side effects, I'd never have given it to her."

"I know," I said. "This is my fault. She's my responsibility. I should never have allowed her to do the scan."

The nurse came out. "There's no sign of pneumonia," she said to me. "Her lungs are clear. And we didn't find any indication of arrhythmia, tachycardia, or stroke."

"Then what's wrong with her?"

"We think it's probably just indigestion, but her symptoms are a bit puzzling."

"The Reminizil," I said.

"No, I checked with the head resident, and that type of drug has never shown any pulmonary or cardiac effects. We're going to keep her for observation overnight," she said, and told us they were transferring her up to a room and that we could see her as soon as she was settled.

While we waited, I called Dave. There was no answer. I left a voice message and then texted him, and by the time I'd done that, Lassiter had come back and a nurse had arrived to show us the way up to Grandma Elving's room.

We could have found it by ourselves. It was on the second floor, directly across from the elevator. Grandma Elving was lying in a hospital bed, hooked up to oxygen and IV and looking even more frail and birdlike than usual, and I felt even guiltier than before, but as soon as she saw us, she pushed the bed up to a sitting position, and said, "I was afraid they weren't going to let you in. I told them I had something extremely important to tell you. Sit down."

"You should be resting," I said, "not—"

"Sit down."

We sat. "I wanted to tell you I remembered the thing I remembered the other day, before Sloane came along and knocked it out of my head. I was thinking about it tonight, trying to remember, and I looked out the window at the snow and it all came back, just like that. It was a Friday, the last Friday before Christmas, and I picked up my pay and put on my coat and went down and bought the camel and Balthazar— you know, the wise man with the casket of myrrh," she said, her words tumbling out in a rush, "They were the last figures I needed, and I ran up to the lunch counter to show them to Marty, and Ralph said he hadn't come into work, and I said, 'He's not sick, is he?' and he said, 'I don't know,' and I thought, *I'll have to show him tomorrow*, and went over to the front door to see if the bus was there, and right then it started to snow. And someone touched me on the shoulder—"

Like I did to Lassiter that day, I thought.

"It was Ralph, and he said, 'We just got a call. Marty's dead.'"

I reached for her hand. "Oh, Grandma Elving, I'm so sorry—"

"I just stood there," she went on, "staring at the snow and the Christmas lights and thinking how ironic it was that the wise man I was holding was the one with the casket of myrrh. Myrrh's a symbol of death, you know," she said. "Ralph told me Marty'd been killed on his way to work."

"How?" Lassiter asked.

"I don't remember," she said, frowning. "And I don't remember what I said to Ralph or what happened after that. Or how I got home. I just remember the snow and Bing Crosby singing 'Silver Bells' and Ralph saying, 'He's dead.' Ralph still had his apron on. And his hairnet."

And there's your trauma, complete with irrelevant details. You were right, Lassiter, it was a TFBM, I thought, sorrier than ever that I'd let Lassiter give her the Reminizil. Even if it hadn't caused a heart attack (and I wasn't at all sure it hadn't) it had done enormous damage. It had brought back the loss of someone she'd obviously been in love with. And ruined the happy Christmas memory she'd been talking about for years.

Lassiter was looking just as stricken as I felt. "Mrs. Elving, I am so sorry," he said.

"No, no," she said, patting his hand. "I'm glad I remembered. Marty was such a lovely boy, and I was so much in love with him." She sighed. "I knew there was something there, all those years, but I just couldn't remember what it was. I suppose I was—what's the word?—suppressing it because it was so sad."

"Repressing it," Lassiter corrected automatically.

"Repressing it, and it was weighing on me," she said. "I feel so much better now that I remember," though I didn't see how that was possible. If the memory of Marty's death had been so traumatic that she'd buried it all these years, how could remembering it not be devastating?

But if it was, she was hiding it well. "Now Lassiter can finish his project," she said happily.

I looked sharply at her, reminded of something she'd said before, not about Lassiter's project, but about...what was it? We'd been in Starbucks, and she'd said she wanted to go see the lights at the Civic Center.

I stared at the IV stand next to her bed, trying to remember. She'd said she thought seeing the lights might make her remember the thing that was eluding her, and I'd thought, *No, she doesn't. She wants—*

"*Here* you are," Dave said, appearing in the doorway. "Ori called me. Are you all right?" and before she could answer him, Sloane came in, too, demanding, "Why didn't you call *me* if you felt sick, Grandma Elving, instead of bothering Ori?" and Jillian, saying, "Oh, I hope they'll let you out tomorrow. My Christmas dinner—," and a nurse who came in to tell us there were too many visitors in the room and Grandma Elving needed to rest.

"I'm going," I told the nurse. "Tell her I'll be here tomorrow to take her home," and went down to the lobby to call that Uber.

But when I called the hospital in the morning to find out what time Grandma Elving was being released, they told me they were keeping her another day to run more tests, which sounded ominous, though when I called her, she wasn't upset at all. "This means I don't have to go to that dreadful dinner of Jillian's. Even hospital food's better than those disgusting things she serves."

"Can I bring you anything?" I asked her. "Like your robe and slippers?"

"No, I don't need anything. You go to dinner at your stepfather's. Lassiter was here this morning and I told him the same thing. The last thing I want is for you two to have to spend Christmas stuck at the hospital with an old lady. I want you to enjoy the holiday."

Watching Sloane paw Lassiter was hardly my idea of enjoyment, but arguing with her wouldn't get me anywhere. I decided to ignore her. I texted Dave and told him I couldn't come to dinner, that I was going to be at the hospital with Grandma Elving, and then went to the grocery store and bought her a poinsettia and a jar of mixed nuts, which I hoped I could talk a nurse into sticking in the microwave for me.

Then, in spite of what she'd said, I drove to her apartment to get her robe and slippers and a couple of nightgowns so she wouldn't have to wear those awful backless hospital gowns.

I still had her keys. I let myself in and went into her bedroom. I gathered up her robe and slippers and then pulled open the top drawer of her bureau to look for a nightgown. And stopped, staring.

There, half-hidden under a stack of neatly folded scarves, was a jumble of painted plaster figures—a camel, a shepherd, a bunch of sheep, a wise man carrying a gold box.

She hadn't lost them. They'd been here all along, displayed on top of the coffee table or on the bookshelf. Until I—or Lassiter—had said we were coming right over.

I stood there a long minute, looking down at the garishly painted figures and considering the implications of them being there, and then grabbed Mary and Balthazar, stuck them in my coat pockets, and took off for the hospital.

"What are you doing here?" Grandma Elving demanded when I came into her hospital room. "Why aren't you over at Jillian's having dinner?"

I plunked Mary and the wise man down on the tray across her bed. "I found these at your apartment," I said. "In your scarf drawer."

"You did?" she said. "Oh, my, I thought they were lost for good. I must have tucked them away in there and then forgotten where I put them. That's what old age does to you. Your memory—"

"You didn't tuck them away," I said furiously. "You dumped them in there last night so Lassiter and I wouldn't see them. That's why you were out of breath when I got there. You *lied* about them getting lost when you moved, about Jillian's having thrown them out! Why?" I asked, hoping against hope there was an innocent explanation for what she'd done—even though I knew exactly why she'd done it.

And I was right. "I just thought looking for them would be a good way for you two to spend some time together without me tagging along like I did when we went downtown," she said. "What's that old saying? Three's a crowd?" She smiled. "That Christmas I worked at Woolworth's there was a boy Alice liked, and I was sure that if he just had a chance to spend some time with her and get to know her, he'd like her, too, but they worked in different departments. 'Make up some excuse to go talk to him,' I told her. 'It'll be Christmas in a few weeks, and you'll never see him again. This is your only chance. Tell him you need change—or ask him for a knife to cut boxes with or something,' but she was just like you, she didn't think he could possibly like her. No self-confidence. She wouldn't do what I told her, and he ended up asking out a girl in Housewares instead, and Alice was heartbroken. So when I saw the same thing happening to you—"

"You decided to play matchmaker," I said.

"Of course not," she said indignantly. "I just thought if the two of you spent a little time together—"

Time together. I thought about her suggesting we take her all those places—Sixteenth Street and the old store and Civic Center—supposedly to jog her memory, and about her leaving us alone in Starbucks while she supposedly went to the bathroom.

"And it would have worked, too," she said, "if that awful Sloane hadn't come along and ruined everything."

"So you faked a heart attack," I said. "Didn't you?" And of course she had. She'd called the two of us, not Dave, and insisted we take her to the emergency room together so he'd have to bring me back to her apartment to get my car, and we'd have to spend more time alone together.

"I never said it was a heart attack," she was saying. "I said I was having chest pains, which I was.

I have them all the time. Dr. Riordan says they're indigestion, but they *might* have been a heart attack. Or pneumonia, especially since Sloane let me sit there in the snow for ages while she flirted with Lassiter. I wouldn't trust her to take care of a parakeet, let alone an old woman. Speaking of which, did you know Woolworth's sold parakeets? They were the cutest things, blue and green and yellow. They sold guinea pigs, too. And turtles with 'Merry Christmas' painted on their backs."

"Don't change the subject," I snapped. "You lied about having a heart attack, you lied about the nativity figures. What else did you lie about? Did you invent that whole story about working at Woolworth's?"

"Of course I didn't," she said. "I just embellished it a little."

"*Embellished* it?" I said, horrified. "Embellished it how?" But I already knew. "Oh, my God, there wasn't any Marty, was there? You made him up."

"No. He really did work at the lunch counter, and he really did say that about my being deadlier than the missile program."

"But he didn't buy you the wise men," I said. "And he wasn't killed."

"No. But Lassiter was so *convinced* something traumatic had to have happened, and I was afraid—"

"That he'd decide your memory wasn't a TFBM if you didn't come up with a trauma, and he'd stop using you as a research subject and spoil your little matchmaking scheme."

She nodded. "You two were getting along so well, it seemed a shame to spoil it."

"So you invented a trauma for him. Which means his research is based on a lie," I said sickly. "Oh, Grandma Elving, this is terrible! What you've done is *wrong!*"

"Nonsense," she said. "Most of what I told Lassiter was true. I *did* work at Woolworth's and so did Marty. And all's fair in love and war."

"But not in science! Don't you understand? You can't just make things up! You falsified data, and he based his theory on that data, so it's invalid, too."

"Just the part about what causes flashbulb memories," she said maddeningly, "not the rest of it. I did have a flashbulb memory, just not the kind that's caused by a trauma."

"That's the only kind there is!" I shouted, and then stopped, looking hard at her, thinking about the implication of what she'd said. "You know what caused your memory, don't you?" I remembered her grasping Lassiter's hand in gratitude after the scan. "You've known since that day he gave you the Reminizil."

"Oh, no. The Reminizil didn't have anything to do with it. I've always known."

"And it wasn't a trauma."

"No."

"But you told Lassiter it was, which means his whole theory's based on a fabrication!" *And I have to tell him*, I thought.

I snatched Mary and Balthazar off the bed table, stuck them back in my coat pockets, and took off for my stepfather's before Grandma Elving could come up with any more excuses. Maybe there'd still be time for him to find another research subject.

It's too late, I thought. *There's only a week left before his project's due.* But I still had to tell him. I couldn't let him turn in research I knew was based on falsified data. Even though it meant he'd probably never speak to me again after I told him.

I'd hoped I could get to Dave and Jillian's before they sat down to dinner and take Lassiter off to one of the bedrooms and tell him, but they were already at the table, eating a dark brown salad with what looked like tentacles.

"I'm sorry to interrupt," I said, "but—"

"In *my* day," Aunt Mildred said, "people knew the importance of punctuality. They didn't just barge in halfway through the meal and ruin everyone's Christmas dinner!"

Like I'm about to do, I thought, looking at Lassiter.

"If the hostess said dinner was at six," Aunt Mildred said, "the guests knew to arrive at five-thirty, not—"

"What's wrong?" Lassiter said, interrupting her. He stood up. "Has something happened?"

Yes, I thought. *Something awful.*

"Did she have another episode?" he demanded.

"No, she's fine," I said. *You have no idea how fine.*

"She's getting out tomorrow."

"Oh, good."

"That's wonderful news!" Dave cut in. "That means you can join us for dinner after all. Gabriela," he said to the maid, "get Ori a chair and a place setting. Lassiter, sit down. Gabriela, bring Ori a—what did you call the salad, Jullian?"

"Hyoki julienne with calamari."

"Bring Ori a calamari salad, and Ori, sit down and join us."

"No, I can't—" I said. "Lassiter, could I talk to you for a minute?" I gestured toward the living room.

"Sure," he said, and started to stand up again.

"Oh, but Gabriela was about to serve the *partridges au poirier*," Jillian said, "and they're very delicate. If they're not served at exactly the right moment, they're ruined."

"Oh, we can't have ruined partridge," Dave said jovially. "Ori, can't whatever you need to tell Lassiter wait till after dinner? Or after the entree at least?"

Jillian didn't wait for me to answer. She said, "Gabriela, bring in the *partridges au poirier*," and there was nothing for it but to sit down and eat the brown salad the maid had plunked down in front of me.

In a way I was grateful—for the delay, not the salad, which tasted just the way it looked. And not for the *partridges au poirier*, which looked like shrivelled-up pigeons on a bed of twigs and were accompanied by a tirade from Aunt Mildred on the subject of how in *her* day when people were invited to Christmas dinner, they wouldn't have *dreamed* of showing up wearing jeans.

But even though the tirade was directed at me, I appreciated having time to collect myself and try to think of some way to break the news that his project was invalid to Lassiter gently.

Who was I kidding? There was no good way to tell him. However I did it, I was going to ruin his Christmas—and probably his life. He'd fail his class and maybe lose his assistantship. *And he'll never talk to me again. He'll think I was in on it with Grandmas Elving—*

"In *my* day, when they admitted you to the hospital, they *kept* you for weeks," Aunt Mildred was saying, "none of this sending you home in a couple of—"

Jillian cut her off. "Sloane was just telling us about the reception she and Lassiter are going to tonight," she said. "At the Dean's house."

"Yes," Sloane said. "In honor of Dr. Bastock. They never invite graduate students, but Dr. Riordan told Dr. Bastock about Lassiter's project and showed him his preliminary findings, and he wants to meet him." She looked proudly at him. "Dr. Riordan said he's a shoo-in for the Rutherman Fellowship. Just think, that stupid story of Grandma Elving's is finally good for something. The reception starts at eight, so we won't be able to stay for dessert."

I looked up sharply. They couldn't leave before—

"Oh, but we're having anise souffle," Jillian said. "With cardamom sauce."

"I know," Sloane said, "but it can't be helped. In fact we should be leaving now, if we don't want to get caught in traffic."

"No," I said, dropping my fork with a clatter. "You can't go yet, Lassiter. I have something I have to tell you."

"Whatever it is," Sloane said, "it'll have to wait. We need to go, don't we, Lassiter?"

He ignored her. "Did Mrs. Elving remember something else?" he asked eagerly, and I thought, *I can't do this. I can't ruin your career—*

"We're already late, Lassiter," Sloane said, and pushed her chair back. "Come on." She glared at him. "Whatever it is, Ori, you can tell him later. Come *on*, Lassiter."

There was no time to lead up to it gently. *I am so sorry, Lassiter*, I said silently, and pulled the Mary and Balthazar out of my pocket and set them on the table in front of him.

"You found a set," he said. "That's wonderful. Have you shown them to Grandma Elving yet? What did she say?" he asked eagerly. "Were they able to trigger her memory of how Marty died?"

"He didn't die," I said. "And I didn't find them. I mean, I did, but not in an antique store. They were at Grandma Elving's. She had them all along. She'd hidden them in a drawer in her bedroom. She lied about them, and about Marty's being killed. There was no thwarted romance, no tragedy that Christmas. She invented the whole thing."

"But she can't have—" Lassiter said. "Are you sure?"

I nodded. "When I showed her the nativity figures, she admitted it."

"I *knew* it," Sloane said, looking at Dave. "We'd all gotten sick of listening to her stupid story about working at Woolworth's, so she decided she had to find some other victim to tell it to."

Which was probably partly true, and I wondered for a split-second if I could say yes, that was why she'd done it: because she was desperate to find someone who'd listen to her.

But Lassiter was convinced an obsessive need to share the account was a sign of a TFBM. He'd be more convinced than ever that there was a tragic event at the core of her memory. I had to tell him the real reason, no matter how humiliating it was.

I took a ragged breath and said, "That wasn't why Grandma Elving did it. She was trying to fix me up with you. She thought if you and I had a chance to spend some time together—"

"Trying to fix *you* up?" Sloane said and gave a hoot of laughter. "You're kidding! As if Lassiter would ever dream of looking at someone as pathetic as you!"

"The point *is*," I went on doggedly, "there wasn't any trauma, Lassiter. She invented it. Her memory wasn't a TFBM. I'm so sorry," I said, watching his face. "I know how important this project was to you."

"What do you mean, *was?*" Sloane demanded.

"She means I can't turn in research based on false data," Lassiter said.

"Why not?" she said. "Can't you just pretend you didn't know it was false?"

"No."

"But what about the fellowship? You wouldn't have to *lie*. You could just not say anything till after they give it to you and then tell them you only just found out that she wasn't telling the truth—"

"That wouldn't be ethical."

"But this wasn't your fault!" She turned and pointed at me. "It was *yours*. If you hadn't told him—"

"She had to tell me," he said to Sloane, and to me, "You're sure about this? Remember we talked about denial and about constructing screen memories and alternative motives to keep from having to confront a memory too painful to face? You're certain that's not what Grandma Elving was doing?"

I wished with all my heart I could say I wasn't. "I'm certain," I said. "She said—"

Sloane interrupted me. "How do you know she's telling the truth, that she didn't just invent this supposed confession of Grandma Elving's so you'd have to go dashing off with her again? How do you know she didn't cook up this whole matchmaking thing herself? She knew she could never get a boyfriend of her own, so she decided to try to steal mine." She turned to look at Dave. "Mother was right. This is what happens when you invite riff-raff you're not even related to to dinner."

"Sloane," Dave said warningly. "Ori, Lassiter, sit down. Let's all discuss this like adults."

Lassiter ignored him. "What exactly did she say?" he asked me.

"She said you were wrong," I told him, "that she knew perfectly well what caused the memory, that she'd known all along, and it wasn't a trauma."

"Did she tell you what *did* cause it?"

I shook my head.

"Come on," he said, standing up. "We've got to go talk to her."

"*Go?*" Sloane said, grabbing his arm. "You can't just go off to the hospital like this. What about the reception? And Dr. Bastock?"

"And my anise souffle?" Jillian said. "It falls if it's not served immediately."

Lassiter ignored them. "Where's your coat?" he asked me brusquely.

"In the hall," I said.

"Lassiter!" Sloane wailed, and Aunt Mildred said, "In *my* day, people didn't walk away from the table without so much as a by your leave and certainly not without—"

I didn't hear the rest of it because Lassiter had already flung my coat at me, hustled me out of the house and into his car, and taken off for the hospital just as he had that night we took Grandma Elving in. He was just as silent as he had been that night, too, his hands clamped to the steering wheel, his eyes fixed on the road.

I waited till we had turned onto Colfax and then asked timidly, "Is it too late for you to redo the project with a different subject?"

"Yes," he said grimly, his eyes on the traffic. "There's no time to run all the tests again. And even if there was, where would you suggest I find somebody else? People with TFBMs are few and far between."

I know one, I thought, remembering the awful moment I'd put those figurines on the table and dashed all his hopes. The look in his eyes as I told him Grandma Elving had lied was something I'd never forget. It was branded into my brain, just like he'd said, irrelevant details and all. I could imagine myself years from now boring people at Dave's family dinners with the story of "that Christmas I destroyed Lassiter Gaines's chances to get the Rutherman Fellowship and my own chance at happiness," telling everyone about Jillian's squid salad and partridges au pear tree and Aunt Mildred's criticisms, trying to exorcise the trauma of having ruined everything.

"If it'll help," I said, "I'll be happy to tell Dr. Riordan what happened," but he wasn't listening.

"It doesn't make any sense," he said. "She told you she made up the story about Marty, but the TFBM signature was there on that scan. I saw it. And the only thing that could have produced that signature is a trauma."

"Unless she faked that, too," I said unhappily. "She faked the story of what happened to Marty and she faked her heart attack. Maybe she faked the trauma, too."

He turned his gaze from the road ahead to me. "What do you mean?"

"She told me she knew you were convinced there had to be a trauma, so she made up one. Maybe she made sure you saw one on the scan, too."

"That's impossible. Lying about her symptoms is one thing, but faking test results is something else entirely. She couldn't fool her EKG at the hospital—you heard her doctor; he said there was no sign of arrhythmia or tachycardia on it—and she definitely couldn't fool a CT-LLI either."

"Unless she thought of the Twin Towers or the *Challenger* instead of Woolworth's when you gave her the Reminizil. Remember how she was worried it might act like a truth serum?"

"Yes," he admitted. "She asked me if the scan would know what she was thinking."

"Because she didn't want you to know she was thinking about something other than Woolworth's."

"Oh, my God, that must have been it, and that was why there wasn't any activation of the stress indicators. I should have known it wasn't a TFBM when I saw that readout," he said. "But it never occurred to me that—"

"Old ladies could be so devious?" I said. "I know."

We were at the hospital. He pulled into the parking garage and parked. "This isn't your fault," I said, getting out of the car. "It's mine. I should have suspected—"

"No, it's not your fault," he said as we went inside and over to the elevators. "If it's anybody's fault, it's mine." We got in the elevator. "But none of this makes any sense. That TFBM signature was on the first scan, too, and that was before she had any way of knowing what I was looking for. That means there *was* a trauma, after all, and she's lying to herself."

Like you are, I thought, following him over to the elevators and up to the second floor. He was doing exactly what I'd done after I found the nativity set in Grandma Elving's bureau, desperately trying to think of some alternative explanation.

But there isn't one, and Grandma Elving's going to tell you that, I thought, and almost bolted as the elevator door opened, but Lassiter took my arm and hustled me across the corridor to her room.

Grandma Elving was sitting up in bed eating turkey and stuffing. "Ori, I told you not to tell him—"

"She was right to tell me," Lassiter said. "You can't base scientific results on false data." He looked hard at her. "*Was* it false?"

"Do you mean, was Marty killed on his way to work?" she asked. "No, but everything else I told you was true. I *was* in love with him. I was in love with all the boys who worked there—Marty and Ralph and Tom and Lamar and Andy. They were all so cute. And I *did* buy Balthazar, and I *did* stand there in the door looking out at the snow," as if that somehow compensated for the lies she'd told. "You had your heart set on something bad having caused the memory, and I knew you wouldn't be satisfied until I came up with one. But nothing bad happened. It was the happiest Christmas of my life."

"But your scan showed the neural signature of a flashbulb memory, and TFBMs are caused by a trauma—"

"Or your theory's wrong," Grandma Elving said, "and something else can cause them. Like happiness."

Lassiter shook his head. "Happiness isn't strong enough or focused enough to produce a flashbulb memory. Only the sudden shock of a trauma is concentrated and powerful enough to trigger one."

"Grandma Elving," I interrupted, "you said you knew what triggered your memory. What was it?"

"I already told you. It was the Friday before Christmas and I bought Balthazar and the camel, just like I said, and then went to the front door to see if my bus was there yet, and I was standing there looking out at the street, at the decorations and the streetlights and all the people hurrying past with their packages and their shopping bags and listening to the sounds of the traffic and Santa's bell and and Bing Crosby singing 'It's Beginning to Look a Lot Like Christmas.' The air coming in from outside was cold, but inside it was warm, and it smelled like popcorn and pine trees and candy canes.

"And as I was standing there, it started to snow," she said, "the flakes falling on the sidewalk and the shoulders of the shoppers and glittering like sequins in the reflection from the streetlamps and the Christmas lights. And as it did, it struck me how beautiful it was and how much I loved it. Not just the snow and the Christmas lights, but all of it—the traffic and the bellringing Santa Claus and the window displays and the lunch counter and the bubble lights and Bing Crosby and the music boxes and parakeets and electric trains and ribbon candy and bubble bath packets and cherry cokes. And waiting on people and giggling with Alice and flirting with the boys who worked there. And this..." she hesitated, as if searching for the right word, "...this *wave* of happiness swept over me. I'll never forget it."

There was no question in my mind that she was telling the truth. You could see it in her face. This, and not some deeply-buried tragedy was what had caused her memory. In spite of the signature neural pattern and the involvement of the amygdala Lassiter had thought he'd seen, her memory wasn't a TFBM.

And it was obvious he knew it, too. His shoulders slumped in defeat, and he said, "It was a happy memory. And you don't tell the story over and over because you're trying to exorcise the trauma. You tell it because you're trying to communicate that feeling of happiness you had to other people."

"Oh, no," she said. "It's not really something you can communicate. I learned a long time ago there was no way to get it across to people. It only bored them."

"Then why do you keep telling it?" I asked curiously.

"It's better than the grumbling most old people do," she said, shrugging, "and I find it's useful for changing the subject when Aunt Mildred begins complaining or Jillian starts in on you." She looked at Lassiter. "I'm sorry I led you to think I was obsessed with remembering it."

"You tried to tell me it was a happy memory," he said. "I should have listened to you. Listen, I need to go. I've got to try and reach Dr. Riordan before he gets to that reception. Ori, do you mind—?"

Finding my own way home? No, I do it all the time. I'll call an Uber. "Of course," I said. "I—"

"No," Grandma Elving said from the bed. "You can't leave yet. Ori, go down to the cafeteria and get me a cup of coffee or—what did you call it? a peppermint latte?—I want to talk to Lassiter alone."

In spite of everything that had happened here tonight, hope flared up in me. *Maybe there is a trauma after all*, I thought, *and it's something she doesn't want me or the family to know, something she can only tell to Lassiter.*

But as I walked across the hall to the elevator, I could hear her saying, "Just because your research didn't prove what you wanted it to doesn't mean it should affect your relationship with Ori."

Oh, no. I pushed the "down" button, willing the elevator to come before Grandma Elving said anything else.

"She's very much in love with you, you know," she said.

I jabbed at the down button again. And again.

"Don't be angry with her," Grandma Elving said. "She didn't know anything about my meddling."

"I'm not angry with her," Lassiter said, and the elevator door finally opened, thank goodness.

It was crammed with people wearing bulky coats and carrying even bulkier packages and stuffed animals and a huge bouquet of silver mylar balloons emblazoned with "Merry Christmas" and "Joy!" and "'Tis the Season."

There was barely room for me, but there was no way I was going to wait for the next one and have to hear Lassiter say, "I'm angry with myself for accidentally giving her the impression we had anything but a professional relationship." Or worse, "Ori? You're kidding!" like Sloane had said.

I lunged into the elevator, pushing my way between the balloon man and a woman with a stuffed plush penguin, willing the door to close, but a man carrying a miniature Christmas tree followed me in, squeezing everyone even closer together, wedging me between the penguin woman and a teenaged-girl in a fur-hooded parka and blocking the door from closing.

"This elevator's going up," the man nearest the elevator panel said, and at the same moment I heard Lassiter say, "I'm angry with myself."

For accidentally giving poor, pathetic Ori the wrong impression, I thought, and said quickly, "Up's fine."

"We're going all the way up to eighth," the man said.

"I'll go up with you and then back down," I said desperately, and reached across the penguin and a woman holding a huge poinsettia to push the "close door" button so I wouldn't have to hear Lassiter tell Grandma Elving how much he pitied me.

I wasn't fast enough. Lassiter was already saying, "I broke the first rule of scientific research: Don't get emotionally involved. Ori tried to tell me that first day that your memory wasn't a TFBM, but I refused to believe her because that would mean I couldn't use you as a subject, and if you weren't a subject, I'd have no excuse to see her again, and I really wanted to see her again—" and the door closed.

I stood there staring blindly at it.

He feels the same way about me that I do about him, I thought, and joy pierced through me like a laser beam, so sharp it was painful and so bright it illuminated everything in the elevator: the red petals of the poinsettia, the gold foil wrapped around its pot, the black velvet bow tie of the penguin, the lighting up of the numbers above the door as we ascended, the jostling silver of the balloons as the man tried to keep them out of everyone's way, all of them intensified and somehow frozen in time.

And not just the images, the sensations: the warmth of the crowded elevator, the tickle of fur against my cheek from the teenager's parka hood, the words of "All I Want for Christmas Is You" and the smells of pine boughs and potting soil and the aftershave someone had no doubt just gotten for Christmas, and I knew that whenever I smelled it for the rest of my life I'd see this moment, this elevator, these people.

I'd thought that the misery I'd felt when I told Lassiter Grandma Elving had lied had been a flashbulb moment, but I'd been wrong. That moment had been painfully vivid, but this one was...indelible. And no wonder Grandma Elving could remember every detail of that Christmas she worked at Woolworth's—it was permanently seared into her amygdala.

Just like the smell of damp wool and the sound of the elevator pinging as it passed floor after floor and the flash of silver from the wayward balloons were in mine.

"Sorry, it's the only kind they allow in the hospital," the man said apologetically to the woman he'd just whacked in the head with them, and she nodded wisely.

"Because of patients who are allergic to latex," she said, and the penguin woman asked the boy standing next to her, "Which room did you say she was in? 821?" and I knew I'd remember that meaningless number, those mundane conversations forever.

Lassiter was wrong, I thought. *Shock and pain and grief aren't the only emotions that can generate a flashbulb memory. Which means Lassiter doesn't have to throw his research out*, and at the thought, I felt an even sharper stab of joy. And relief. I hadn't ruined his chance at the Rutherford Fellowship. I hadn't ruined his life.

I have to tell him before he calls Dr. Riordan, I thought, and lunged for the floor-buttons panel, but there was no way to reach it. There were too many people in the way, plus the Christmas tree. And the damned balloons.

"I have to get off," I called to the man who'd been pushing buttons before. "Can you push 'two' for me? Please? It's an emergency!"

"I told you, we're going up," he said. "We're already to four," and I had to wait impatiently as the floor numbers—four, five, six—lit up in turn, hoping someone, anyone, would get off before the eighth floor and I could take the stairs down.

Nobody did, and when we finally reached it, it took forever for everyone to get off. *It'll be faster to take the elevator than the stairs*, I thought, but before the door could close the elevator filled with people going home, mashing me against the back wall so I couldn't get off, and then stopped at every single floor on the way down.

It seemed like hours before we finally got back to the second floor and I was able to manhandle my way out of the elevator and run across to Grandma Elving's room.

Lassiter wasn't there. "He left," she said. "He—"

But I didn't wait to hear why, or for the elevator to come back. I ran to the stairway, pushed the door open, and racketed down the steps to the ground floor, and out to the parking garage, praying Lassiter's car would still be there.

It was, but Lassiter wasn't in it. I stared at it blankly for a minute, and then started back along the row of cars to the door to the hospital, trying to think where Lassiter might be. Grandma Elving had said he'd left. Had he gone down to the lobby to call Dr. Riordan or—?

The door opened and Lassiter came out, scanning the concrete pillars and the rows of cars.

"What are you doing out here?" he said. "I've been looking for you everywhere. I wanted to tell you—"

"I've got something to tell you, too," I said breathlessly. "Grandma Elving was right. Your theory's wrong. TFBMs—"

"I don't care about the TFBMs. Or Dr. Bastock and the Rutherford Fellowship or any of it. What I care about is you."

"I know," I said impatiently. "I love you, too. But you have to listen. Your project—"

"I told you, I don't care about the project or the fact that your grandmother lied to me or that I have to start over."

"But you don't have to start over. That's what I've been trying to tell you," I said, but he wasn't listening.

"Setbacks happen all the time in science. They're a natural part of it. I'll just have to find a subject who's actually had a TFBM, that's all, or find some undergrads who are willing to watch horror movies. Or maybe we can get your grandmother to tell us how she faked that CT-LLI scan and what she was really thinking about during it, and see if *that's* a TFBM."

"No," I said. "You don't understand. She wasn't faking. She wasn't thinking about a trauma. She was thinking about that Christmas she worked at Woolworth's. That's what I've been trying to tell you! Her memory *was* a TFBM. Not the 'T' part—there wasn't any trauma—but the flashbulb part. Your theory was wrong. Traumas aren't the only thing that causes flashbulb memories. They can be caused by positive emotions, too."

"Look, I know you're trying to cheer me up, but—"

"*No*," I said. "It's true. I know because I just had one. In the elevator." I explained what had happened and how it had had all the earmarks of a flashbulb moment—the clarity and intensity, the full sensory involvement, the irrelevant details.

"But the research has shown happiness not only isn't strong enough to produce a flashbulb moment, it doesn't activate the amygdala or the hippocampus, it activates the limbic cortex."

"I know, but I'm not talking about happiness. I'm talking about joy, which is a totally different emotion. People think of them as the same thing because they're both positive emotions, but I don't think they are. Happiness is a warm, pleasant, all-over kind of feeling. Joy's nothing like that. It pierces right through you, and it's so intense, it's almost painful, and I think that's the kind of experience Grandma Elving had standing there, looking out the door at the snow, a sort of..." I faltered, groping for the right word.

"Epiphany," Lassiter said. "Like the wise men had when they saw the star."

"Yes, exactly," I said. "And I'll bet if you put those wise men under a CT-LLI scan and asked them to tell you about it, the scan would look just like Grandma Elving's scan. And a TFBM."

"Unfortunately, they're not available," Lassiter said, grinning. "Unless you still have their plaster counterparts on you." He turned serious. "But you are. Would you be willing to let me take you to the lab and run a scan on your elevator moment? I know it's Christmas, but—"

"I'd be glad to," I said. "As long as you take me out to dinner afterwards. But not to Dave and Jillian's. I can't face another one of her squid salads."

"Me neither," he said. "How about someplace romantic? Like Starbucks?"

"That sounds perfect," I said.

He tucked my arm through his, and we started down the concrete garage to his car. Halfway there, he stopped and said, "We're going to be stuck going to dinner there and putting up with Sloane and her mother every year, aren't we?"

He's going to have a whole bunch of my flash-bulb moments to choose from if he keeps this up, I thought.

"Yes," I said, "but don't worry. My dad gets a new wife every five years or so, and in the meantime, Grandma Elving will be there to run interference for us. If you're lucky, she might even tell you the story about that Christmas she worked at Woolworth's."